HAVE YOU EVER SEEN
A JACKALOPE ?

HAVE YOU EVER SEEN A JACKALOPE ?

JILLIAN LUND

The RGU Group ◆ Tempe, Arizona

For Mackenzie,
who is everything nice.

-Auntie Jill

The illustrations were rendered in acrylic
on cold-press illustration board.
The text type was set in Giovanni Book
The display type was set in Candy Randy
Composed in the United States of America
Graphic layout by Adriana Patricia De La Roche
Production supervision by Denise Young

Printed in China

First impression

Library of Congress Catalog Number: 2003093747—Hardcover

International Standard Book Number: 1-891795-11-2—Hardcover

The RGU Group

www.theRGUgroup.com

10 9 8 7 6 5 4 3 2 1 (hc)

One fine day in the Wild, Wild West, a kangaroo rat named Cody met an animal unlike any he had seen before.

The strange animal looked Cody up and down and said, "Tell me, friend – have you ever seen a Jackalope?"

"A Jackalope?" said Cody. "Hmmm. Nope. I ain't never heard o' such a thang. What sort o' critter is it?"

"Oh, it's a sight to see, a real treat," the animal said. "The Jackalope is smart and good-lookin', too. I guess I'd say it's about the most wonderful beastie you could ever behold. Well, got to skedaddle. Have a nice day."

And just as quick as it might take you to say *whatsa-mahoozle-doodle*, the stranger was gone, leaving the kangaroo rat with a big curiosity.

"Well, hot-diggity-chili-dog!" thought Cody. "I wonder if anybody in these parts can tell me more about this Jackalope feller."

So off he hopped until he met a white-winged dove.

"Have you ever seen a Jackalope?" asked Cody.

"I've heard it builds a mighty fine nest," the dove coo'd from her perch.

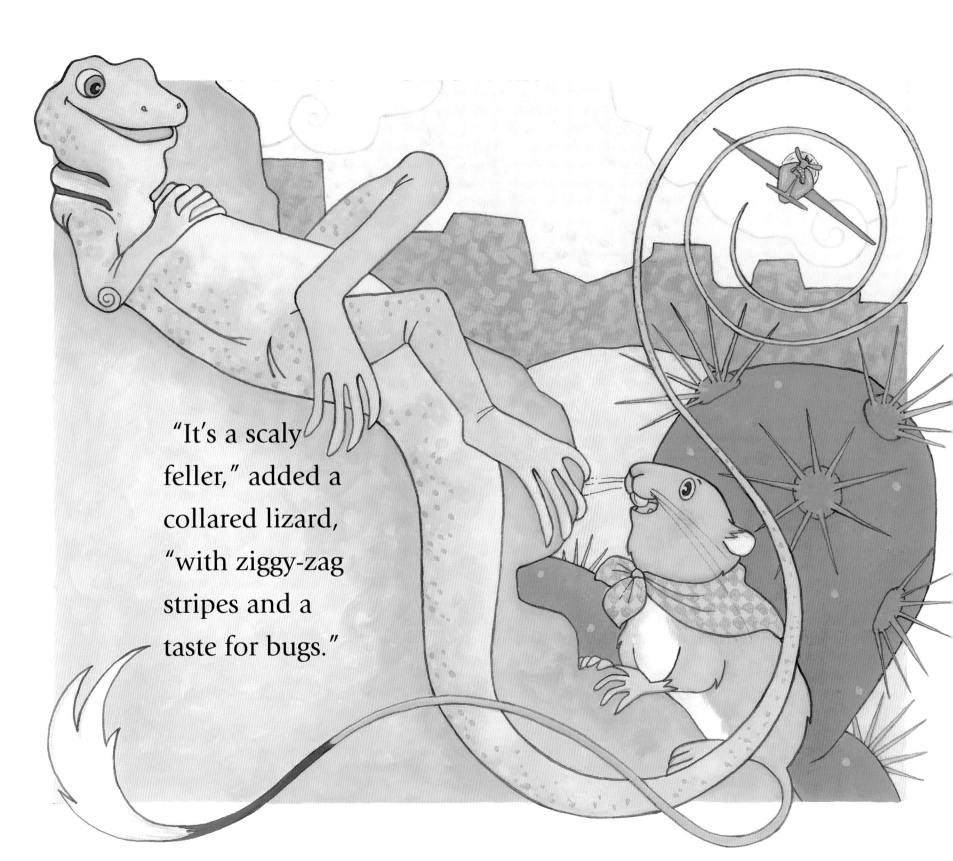

"It's a scaly feller," added a collared lizard, "with ziggy-zag stripes and a taste for bugs."

"So it's good-lookin' and stripey and has bug breath," thought Cody. "That puts me to mind o' my uncle Ned, 'cept for the good-lookin' part."

He continued on until he met several other critters he knew.

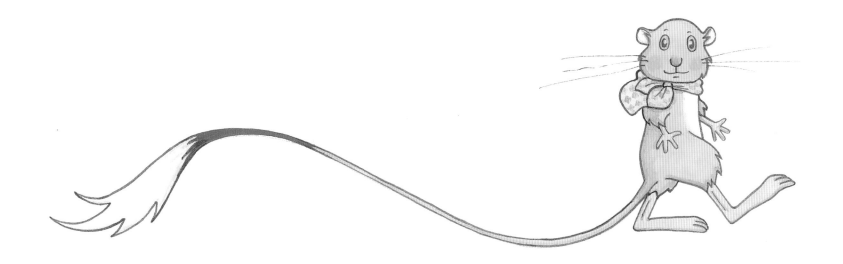

"What can you fellers tell
me about a Jackalope?"

"It's near invisible when it's sittin' still," said the scorpion, "and it has a mean sting!"

"Poor little feller's only got ten legs," said the centipede.

"It smells as purty as a field full o' poppies," said the skunk. "Just like me."

"It's always lookin'
fer an easy meal," said
the turkey vulture. Cody
quickly moved along.

"It's mighty fast!"
said the roadrunner.
"Like a bolt o' lightnin'."

The handsome quail said, "It takes good care o' its young'uns."

"It's a homey feller. Likes to stay indoors," was all the old tortoise had to say.

The afternoon sun was beginning to lie low in the sky as Cody hopped up a mesa. "Have any of y'all ever seen a Jackalope?"

"I've heard tell it's got big yeller teeth," said the coyote.

"And big yeller eyes!" hooted the elf owl.

"So it's smart, good-lookin' and stripey," Cody thought. "It has bug breath, is near invisible, has a hurtful sting and ten legs. It smells like a skunk, likes kids, is always hungry, and is a speedy feller. It's a real homebody with yeller teeth and yeller eyes.

"This has got to be the strangest critter ever to be sighted west o' the Mississippi!" he exclaimed. "I cain't figure out why I ain't never seen somethin' so ding-dang-darned interestin' before!"

"Thatsss because it'sss a myth," hissed a king snake, lying on a nearby rock. "Jackalopesss sssimply do not exissst."

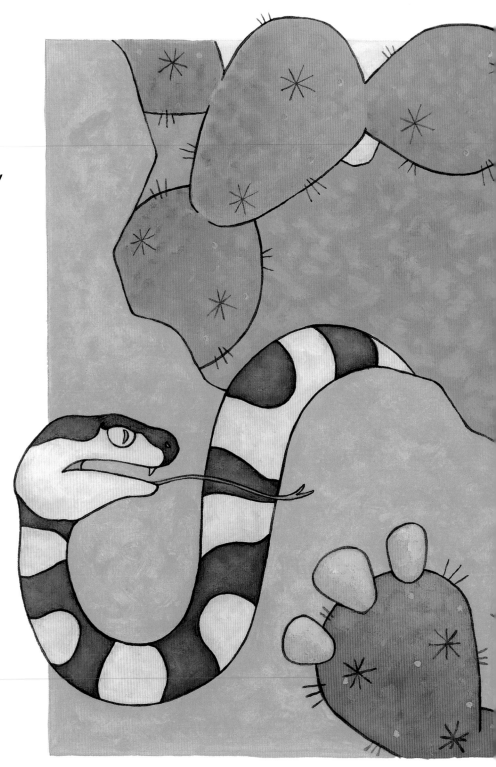

Cody headed for home. "Oh well!" he sighed. "I was sure lookin' forward to meetin' one. I guess that feller I met this mornin' was just pullin' my leg."

"I guess he was at that," chuckled the Jackalope, as he hopped off into the sunset.

GREAT SOUTHWESTERN JACKALOPE

Is it a jackrabbit? A pronghorned antelope? No – it's a Great Southwestern Jackalope, a rare – and rarely seen - creature that looks a little like both! The Great Southwestern Jackalope – seen in this book - is one of two kinds of jackalope found in the western United States. The Great Southwestern has horns that are forked in the middle, which allows it to pry fruit off the prickly pear cactus – its favorite thing to eat. The Jackalope's coat is usually golden or honey-brown, enabling it to blend easily into its western desert surroundings. Jackalopes have a tendency to appear in unexpected places, doing unexpected things – in fact, it's said that they'll try anything at least once! They're very speedy, full of mischief, and hate being seen, so if you spot one it's only because it allowed you to.

Some people claim that the Jackalope is a myth. Others swear they've seen a Jackalope just out of the corner of their eye, hopping off into the sunsets of the great American West.

BANNER-TAILED KANGAROO RAT

Kangaroo Rats hop like kangaroos on powerful hind legs, which is how they got their name, but they are not related to kangaroos directly, except that both are mammals. Cody, our curious kangaroo rat, is only 12-15 inches long, and that includes his 9-inch tail, which looks like a paintbrush that was dipped in white paint. Kangaroo rats take sandbaths and communicate by foot-drumming and kicking sand. They also have been known to growl, squeak and even chuckle.

Their diet includes leaves, seeds, stems, buds, insects and some fruit. The Banner-Tailed Kangaroo Rat lives underground in large sandy mounds of complex tunnels that may be as long as 70 feet and have several entrances and exits. It is nocturnal, which means it only leaves its home at night - when the desert has cooled - to look for food. Cody, however, never seems to have enough time, so he often goes out during the day as well. Banner-Tailed Kangaroo Rats can be found in western Texas, southeastern Arizona and southern New Mexico.